QUANTUM (

Conn Iggulden is one of the most successful authors
of historical fiction writing today. His two No. 1 bestselling series, on Julius Caesar and on the Mongol
Khans of Central Asia, tell the stories of how the
greatest empires of their day began.

Conn Iggulden is co-author of *The Dangerous Book for
Boys*. He lives in Hertfordshire with his wife and their
children.

www.conniggulden.com

Also by Conn Iggulden

THE EMPEROR SERIES
The Gates of Rome
The Death of Kings
The Field of Swords
The Gods of War

THE CONQUEROR SERIES
Wolf of the Plains
Lords of the Bow
Bones of the Hills
Empire of Silver
Conqueror

Blackwater

BY CONN IGGULDEN AND HAL IGGULDEN
The Dangerous Book for Boys
The Dangerous Book for Boys Yearbook

BY CONN IGGULDEN AND DAVID IGGULDEN
The Dangerous Book of Heroes

BY CONN IGGULDEN AND ILLUSTRATED BY
LIZZY DUNCAN
Tollins: Explosive Tales for Children

CONN IGGULDEN

Quantum of Tweed

The Man with the Nissan Micra

HARPER

HARPER

An imprint of HarperCollins*Publishers*
77–85 Fulham Palace Road,
Hammersmith, London W6 8JB

www.harpercollins.co.uk

A paperback original 2012
1

A catalogue record for this book
is available from the British Library

ISBN 978 0 00 745598 0

Typeset in Sabon by Palimpsest Book Production Limited,
Falkirk, Stirlingshire
Printed and bound in Great Britain by
Clays Ltd, St Ives plc

MIX
Paper from
responsible sources
FSC™ C007454

To Kiera Godfrey

Chapter One

Albert Rossi would be the first to tell you that breaking into the world of professional assassination is no easy task. In almost any job, you are allowed to make the odd mistake, with red faces all round and perhaps a new office nickname. Not so with hit men. If assassins had a theme tune, it would be something solemn and deeply dignified. Adagio in G minor, perhaps. Soft rock would not be appropriate for such a serious business. Bonnie Tyler would not do at all.

It might have helped if Albert had spent his earlier years in the army, becoming a grim and, yes, somewhat suave dealer in death. He did not do this, however, because Albert Rossi was a late starter. Up to the age of forty-nine, his life had proceeded in an aimless fashion, much like the windows of his beloved menswear shop in

Eastcote, Middlesex. Things changed, but things also stayed very much the same. Sadly, his debt to the bank rose every year.

Albert's life took a lurch onto a new path when he was driving home one Monday afternoon. The bank had taken to writing rather unpleasant letters to him and adding £30 to his overdraft for each one. He had tried replying. He had even tried charging them for his own letters. To his horror, this seemed only to encourage them. Lately, he had begun to receive statements with a red border and the word 'bailiff' around line three. Perhaps he was distracted that Monday. The threat of bailiffs will do that to a man.

His car, a Nissan Micra, was also not appropriate for an assassin, but in fairness it was fantastically appropriate for the owner of a men's clothing shop. He may have been listening to Bonnie Tyler, but moments of immense stress often blur details. To this day he cannot remember why he shudders whenever he hears 'Total Eclipse of the Heart'.

The first he knew of his career change was when a small man wearing a poorly cut suit and smart black shoes ran out in front of him. The brakes of the car were excellent, but as Albert panicked, he locked the wheels and skidded. At the moment of impact, the little man *popped* into the air, so quickly and completely that at first Albert dared to hope it hadn't happened at all. To his horror, he saw a smartly shoed foot sliding into view at the top of his windscreen. The little man had ended up on the roof.

In the stunned moment that followed, Albert swallowed nervously. With trembling hands, he turned off the radio – rather than have Bonnie Tyler belt her way through a chorus that could only be slightly sinister in the circumstances. The silence was eerie. The sort of silence that is interrupted by a dead man sliding into view can never be the 'nuns in a reading room' kind. 'Eerie' is very much *it* for the slight squeak of a size-nine brogue on your windshield. It did not help that Albert recognised the brand of socks as one he had marked down to 40 per cent of its full price.

The road was empty, though suburban houses seemed to press in on all sides. There had been the squeal of brakes and the thump. Surely the windows would be positively *filling* with Girl Guides and Miss Marples, noting his number plate and groping for the phone. As Albert stepped out, he was tempted to just push the little fellow off and make a dash for freedom. A man who can sell a jumper with suede strips on the front is made of sterner stuff than that, however.

Albert took hold of a wrist and tried not to look at the rest of the man as he felt for his pulse. There wasn't one. He checked his own wrist for the right spot and couldn't find one there either. It's a lot harder to do than your average medical drama makes it look.

Focusing on the task, Albert did not hear the stranger approach. He felt something poke at his kidneys. Was he being mugged? Honestly, whoever it was could not have *chosen* a worse time.

'Don't turn round,' came a deep voice in his ear. 'Just tell me the name of the man you ran over.'

Albert wondered if he had struck his own head in the accident. Had the air bags gone off? Was it possible not to notice an air bag going off? He made a strangled sound as he tried to peer into the Nissan Micra without moving his head.

'His name,' the voice went on. 'Just that.'

There was a delicate scent of male aftershave in the air, Albert noted dimly. Unlike the voice and his entire day up to that point, it was actually quite nice.

'I . . . I hit him with my car!' Albert said. 'I didn't have time to ask him!'

4

'You expect me to believe it was an accident? You don't know who this is?'

'Look, I'm truly sorry. I was driving along Hawthorn Avenue and . . .'

To his amazement, the man at his ear chuckled.

'Relax, Mr Dangerous Driver. I didn't really think you were a professional. It was so neat, that's all. I was lining up my shot . . . Don't turn round!'

Albert froze all over again. The fact that he was being poked by an actual gun was too much to take in. Could he hear sirens in the distance? No chance. That was another part of real life that the medical dramas had not represented accurately.

On the television, the police were always in the next road, ready to fire up the sirens and arrive in seconds with screeching cars. That did not seem to be the case in Hawthorn Avenue, Eastcote. Albert thought he would be dead on the side of the road by the time the police eventually turned up. He suspected his own expression would be one of total bafflement.

'Look, the police are on their way,' he said, in the complete absence of proof. 'I'm sorry if I made you angry . . .'

'Angry?' The man chortled. He was very jolly for someone in what Albert was beginning to realise was probably not a jolly profession. 'You saved me a job. I wouldn't have bothered with an alibi if I'd known you were going to come along and flatten my target for me.'

Albert suspected he was going into shock. He wasn't *certain* what this entailed, but he was feeling light-headed and faintly nauseous, which probably fitted the bill. He wondered how an assassin would react to having someone throw up on their shoes.

'Will you kill me now?' Albert asked.

'Not for free, old son. You haven't seen my face and you did do me a favour.'

'I could . . . just drive away, in fact?' Albert said, almost pleading. There was silence for a moment.

'If you sneak a single look at me, I'll take it badly, understand? Your number plate is on the road, so I can always find you.'

Albert felt the pressure on his kidneys vanish and he opened the car door with shaking hands. He couldn't look at the body again. Presumably, it would fall off when he built up a respectable speed.

The second important event of that day occurred as Albert tried to start his car and put it into reverse gear *whilst looking determinedly out of the back window*. Perhaps it was fate that led him to accidentally select first gear and run his second man down that morning. The Micra leapt forward eagerly, bumping once, then twice.

Albert gave a cry of appalled despair. He would have driven off if he hadn't remembered his number plate on the road. A black mobile phone was spinning by his front tyre. Next to it was a pistol, complete with silencer. Albert snatched them all up, crunched the car into reverse and then he was off, back down Hawthorn Avenue, leaving the dead behind.

Chapter Two

The police did arrive, in the end. They had received reports of a hit-and-run from a retired teacher named Miss Morrison and one Girl Guide who was home sick from school. The missing number plate had foxed them all, however. Though Albert spent the night waiting for a knock on the door, it did not come. What did come was a call on the new mobile from Stephen Hawking, or someone who sounded very much like him.

'Not as neat as we were expecting,' said a metallic voice. 'You are not paid extra for bystanders.'

Albert could only listen in growing horror as he realised it was not Stephen Hawking at all.

'The money will be left in the usual place,' the voice continued.

At *that very moment*, Albert changed careers.

'No,' he said, suddenly. 'Leave it in the rubbish bin outside Eastcote station at midnight.'

'Very well,' the disguised voice said flatly, which was not too surprising.

Albert switched off the phone, gasping. In all his years of herringbone jackets, of Burlington socks and renting tuxedoes, he had never experienced a *fraction* of the excitement that filled him then.

He wasn't certain when the bins were emptied, so at five minutes past midnight he was there, rummaging in the bin and pulling out a package wrapped in creased brown paper. When he had brought it back to his flat above the shop and opened it with shaking hands, he discovered it held ten thousand pounds.

After finding a charger for his new phone, he'd discovered there were other 'jobs' on offer. He had learned not to refer to them as 'slayings' after Stephen Hawking's initial pained silence. Obviously, by now he knew it wasn't the famous physicist calling him, but it was somehow comforting to imagine the kindly genius there on the other end.

If the bank had been even *slightly* reasonable, Albert would never have accepted. Ten thousand pounds had gone some way to keeping the wolves away, just not far enough. He wondered if every assassin had an overdraft and, for a moment, felt for them as a group before dismissing the idea. No doubt assassins spent their leisure time driving to casinos in Aston Martins. With buxom women, probably, the lucky swine.

After retrieving a file from the same bin, Albert read feverishly about the activities of Peter Schenk, a wealthy and worryingly ruthless businessman. Schenk owned a number of shady operations, from betting shops to a junkyard and a bailiff company. Just reading *that* made Albert want to run him over.

It was the section on hobbies that gave Albert his inspiration. Most weekends Schenk flew a hang-glider over at Dunstable, near Luton. Albert imagined the man drifting past, blissfully unaware, as Albert aimed, fired and kept Eastcote in menswear and golf balls for another decade. It wasn't as if Schenk was a decent old buffer with a fondness for chocolate and cats. The file made it clear that Schenk was every bit as dangerous as those who rested their hopes in Albert Rossi.

On a Saturday morning in June, Albert shut the shop early, having selected a long black coat from the rack – a 10 per cent cashmere mix, one of his best. He placed the coat, gun and phone on the passenger seat of his Micra and set off.

*　*　*

Dunstable is mostly famous for its gliders, those long-winged fibreglass birds that drift over the vast natural ridge with grace and speed. They are winched along the ground until the breeze slips under the wings and they rise aloft. Like huge kites on a string of steel wire, they are flung into the heavens to swoop and soar amongst the clouds. So beautiful are they, so able to shrug off the bonds of gravity and the sullen earth below, that in those first moments of glorious flight you almost forget that what you'd *really* like is a bloody engine.

There is also a sheer cliff to the north of the airfield that attracts those fans of hang-gliding who thrive on risk and adrenalin. Young fliers gallop madly to the edge and throw themselves into space. The delicate wings are toys of the air for a brief time, until they land and have to be walked all the way to the top again.

It was a beautiful, sunny day with the sky a bowl of perfect blue when Albert arrived. He left his Micra in the car park of the gliding club and walked out beyond the buildings. In a sense, he realised, he was leaving civilisation behind. He had murder in his heart and the strong sensation that he should have chosen more appropriate shoes.

Albert saw no sign of his intended victim as

he reached the base of the cliff and began to make his way up. The path he followed wound around the hill, sometimes barely more than a track. Stumbling up it, Albert had his first glimpse of Schenk's hang-glider on the ridge, bright yellow and jerking in the wind as its owner checked every strap before launch.

Albert continued doggedly, peering up at Schenk each time he came into view. Far below, he could see tractors racing across the grass of the airfield to retrieve the gliders as they came to rest. It was a peaceful scene, but he reminded himself that he had not come for tranquillity. He was the angel of death and he set his jaw in what he hoped was a grim expression. Imagine, if you will, the face of a spaniel who has just been given a piece of bread covered in hot Colman's mustard. There, you have it exactly. That was Albert's expression. Admittedly, it was not what he hoped for, but that is often the way with men of a certain age.

When he was close to the top, Albert stopped in frustration. Two bodyguards accompanied his target. They wore dark suits and sunglasses, which was more than enough to let him know their role in Schenk's life. Albert could hardly take aim while they looked on. Shaking with tension, Albert saw a small track leading across the face of the final ridge. He didn't hesitate and edged his way along it, his back pressed to the rough stone, mere inches from the abyss.

The track narrowed until he was convinced a sudden gust would snatch him off. He couldn't turn and the tips of his black Oxford shoes were actually over the edge, with nothing but air below.

Albert was staring upwards as Peter Schenk launched above his head, rising into the blue sky. It was time. Albert tried to draw his gun as Schenk began to race his hang-glider in great swoops, back and forth across the edge of the ridge. The silencer snagged in Albert's coat and he pulled the entire thing over his head in his panic. One last yank revealed the gleaming weapon but sent the coat fluttering down. Albert steadied himself as Schenk came zooming along, drunk on danger and adrenalin.

Albert felt rather the same way himself. He braced one arm with the other and fired until the silenced gun was empty. In response, Schenk brushed a hand across his face as if batting away a wasp. In a rage, Albert considered throwing the gun at him.

At that moment, Schenk looked across and saw Albert on the ledge, halfway up a cliff, as if suspended in mid-air. To his astonishment, Albert waved weakly at him. For an instant, Schenk wavered in his flight. His hand slipped from the control bar and his hang-glider drifted too close to the cliff face. It was then that the yellow wing snagged and tore itself apart. In a heartbeat it went from a swooping bird to a collection of struts and ragged cloth.

Albert watched Peter Schenk spiral all the way down, overcome with something like remorse. His debt to the bank would be reduced, of course, but a man had lost his life to save a menswear shop. Somehow, Albert could not regret it. There had been something quite poignant in the way Schenk waved back at him before falling. Life, Albert reflected, did have a way of catching you unprepared.

Chapter Three

The following morning, Albert stirred from troub-
led sleep to reach out and pick up the phone by
his bed. He had bought the old-fashioned item
in a fanciful mood, then found that a rotary dial
was nowhere near as much fun as he remem
bered. Calling a mobile number took ages. As he
pressed the bulky receiver to his ear, he realised
the ringing was still going on. He leapt out of
bed like a salmon, crossing the room to the still
dusty coat he had retrieved from the bottom of
the cliff. It was the special phone and he tried
to calm his breathing as he took the call.

'Yes, Mr Hawking?' he said, then clapped a
hand over his mouth. There was a long silence
at the other end before he heard the mechanical
voice he knew so well.

'You think this is Stephen Hawking?' the voice

asked. Even through the electronic disguise, Albert could hear the surprise.

'It's my nickname for you, that's all,' he said, wincing.

'It will do. Good work yesterday. For a man known as "Bullet", you are more imaginative than I was told to expect.'

Albert Rossi digested this for a moment, thinking back to the assassin he had run over in his Micra two weeks before.

'I . . . work with whatever is to hand,' he said, trying to sound calm and generally relaxed.

'I have another job. Are you available?'

Albert thought of the money he still owed and the constant drain on his bank account from the general lack of interest in Eastcote menswear. Despite the terror he had experienced on the cliff at Dunstable, despite the sweat that had dribbled into his eyes, he had never felt more *alive*. Cufflinks and bow ties were nowhere near as exciting. Perhaps one day he would even visit a casino – and not just to use the men's room this time.

'Absolutely,' he said. 'Drop the details off with the money. The usual place. Oh, and I'll need some bullets.'

'I see. What kind?'

Albert panicked. There is something about a

pistol that makes grown men want to pick it up. He'd spent part of the previous evening posing with it in front of a mirror. Where had he left the thing? As the voice asked again, he spotted the handle sticking out from under his pillow. Not the handle, the 'grip', he reminded himself. Or possibly the 'butt'; he really had no idea. New sweat broke out on his forehead as he read out the tiny lettering on the gun.

'Um . . . Colt Government 1911. Dot forty-five.'

It was heavy and square in his hand, but he felt more confident just holding it. A Colt 45! A piece of America in an Englishman's hand. Glorious.

'Very well. I'll put a couple of full clips in the envelope.'

Albert was not exactly what you would call a ladies' man. The great flames of youthful passion had passed him by, with the exception of one long summer in his late thirties when he dallied with an attractive widow and had even thought about asking her to marry him. The fires of his heart had turned to ash when he discovered she was also running around with the local butcher. Rather than compete with a man who could woo with sausages, Albert had sent her a dignified letter and ended it. Those golden days were still among his favourite memories, but as the sum total of a man's experiences with the opposite sex, it was somewhat lacking.

Perhaps as a result, the group of teenage girls hanging around the entrance to Eastcote station at midnight left him slightly flustered. As he waited for them to leave, he checked his watch at intervals. They seemed in no hurry and all he could do was stand near the crucial bin and read a newspaper.

He may have had an air of innocence, despite his deadly new profession. It takes time to grow into a hard-faced assassin, even for one who had begun so promisingly. Albert's wide-eyed nervousness may have caught the interest of the girls in the way that a mouse will attract a pack of feline predators; it is hard to say. It may have been the amount of alcohol the girls had consumed or the fact that they had a vague idea of asking a stranger to buy more. Either way, they surrounded him like lions on a wobbly zebra.

They were loud when they screeched with laughter. They were also loud when they whispered. Albert could only cringe and stammer answers as they fired questions at him. When he dropped his newspaper and bent down to pick it up, one of them patted him on the bottom and then was almost sick laughing at his horrified expression.

'You a dirty old man, then?' another asked, grinning.

Albert tried to reply, but to say he was out of his depth is to imply that he had some concept of depth. He was not even in the pool.

'He's got a long coat. I think he *is* a dirty old man.'

Albert knew about blushes, of course. The lady he had once adored had read romantic novels by the yard, though as he reflected later and with justifiable bitterness, not a single one had a butcher as its hero. She had even read a few choice passages aloud to him, perhaps hoping that they would inspire Albert Rossi to similar efforts. Blushes were mentioned every second or third page in those.

He was not as familiar with the wave of heat and embarrassment that seemed to begin at his shoes and work up to the stiff collar of his shirt. He suspected small Eskimo children could warm themselves on him at that moment. In a sort of daze, he imagined they would bless him for saving them from a hard winter and only roll him out on the coldest of days. He could almost see the stern Eskimo mother wagging a finger at the little ones and telling them not to waste their

Albert when it was a mere forty degrees below zero. The mind is a strange thing, and it is worth remembering that Albert was under a lot of stress. With an effort, he shook his head clear of Eskimos.

'I'm just waiting for someone,' he said.

The first girl was perhaps sixteen. She was dressed in a way that was clearly meant to be appealing. There was a lot of flesh spilling out of her top. Most of it jiggled when she laughed and he could hardly point out the chip that had fallen into her cleavage without revealing that he had noticed her cleavage. He decided against that.

'My mum warned me about men like you,' she said cheerfully. 'All they want is sex.'

Albert gaped at her, but he found nerve enough to reply.

'I'd be satisfied with a bit of peace and quiet,' he said firmly. 'It *is* after midnight.'

'Ooh, he wants you to satisfy him, Sal!' her friend hooted. '*Dirty* old man!'

A distant rumble under his feet saved him from worse. One of the girls yelled 'Traaaain!' and the whole painted pack scooted into the station. Albert watched them go with a feeling of relief mingled with regret. He had not talked to a female for a long time. Perhaps if he went to a casino in his new role as assassin-for-hire he would meet some Russian beauty at the roulette table. He shook his head. Unlikely, even for a fantasy.

Now that the street was quiet, he sidled over to the bin at last. Under the half-eaten kebabs and free newspapers was a thick brown envelope, almost a package. It looked bulkier than the one for Peter Schenk, but he didn't want to open it there. He hurried down Field End Road back to his flat, tucking the envelope safely under the gaberdine coat he was wearing for just that purpose. A dirty old man would not have the style to carry off gaberdine wool, he told himself. It would more likely be a blend or, he shuddered at the thought, *textured polyester*.

Standing in the doorway of the kebab shop by the station, holding a large doner with salad, special sauce and a bright green chilli pepper, Police Constable George Thompson watched him go. Despite his profession, PC Thompson was not suspicious by nature. He had been amused at first to see a group of young girls harass a rather prim-looking man over by the station. Yet there was something strange about the man's reactions as he hovered around the bin on the crest of the hill. The police officer had been chewing slowly and deliberately on his doner with only vague interest when he saw Albert Rossi search the bin. That interest had sharpened considerably when he saw the man come up with a thick envelope and go hurrying off down the road with it.

PC Thompson had very blue eyes, weary after a long shift. If Albert had been looking into them, he would have seen them go cold and hard, much like the final piece of the kebab. The policeman was a believer in instinct and he chose to spend his last hour before bed walking slowly along Field End Road after the unsuspecting Albert Rossi, then noting the door number of his little flat on the balcony above the shops.

Chapter Four

Four days later, Albert responded to a knock at the door of his flat. His bed was covered with plans and diagrams, as well as the *Collins Encyclopedia*, volume four: 'De–Es'. He opened the door cheerfully with a piece of buttered toast in his mouth and a cup of tea in his hand. When he saw that his visitor was a uniformed policeman, he choked on the toast so suddenly and violently that PC Thompson seriously considered calling for an ambulance.

After a good ten minutes of pounding Albert Rossi on his back and then supporting his red-faced frame, PC Thompson found himself in a small kitchen, settling the man into a chair and fetching him a glass of water, which Albert sipped while they waited for his eyes to stop bulging.

'Sorry about that,' Albert wheezed. 'Went down the wrong way.'

'Not a problem, sir. Are we feeling better now?'

'*I* am, officer. I don't know about *you*, though.'

Albert smiled in a sickly way, hoping his terror at the sight of a policeman had been put down to inhaling toast and not considered suspicious behaviour. It did not help that this particular policeman looked exactly as Albert Rossi expected policemen to look. He was vaguely aware that they had done away with height restrictions, but PC Thompson was not only tall, he also had a neat and fairly bushy moustache. He was slightly red in the face, too, though Albert had to concede that it might have been from the exercise in the doorway. In short, George Thompson could easily have been cast as the serious, middle-aged policeman in any film about Sherlock Holmes. Albert became increasingly uncomfortable as the man pulled up his own chair and looked around.

'Under normal circumstances, sir, I would have asked you to invite me in for a chat. I'm not sure you ever did that, with all the choking going on.'

Albert waved the idea away. He hoped the gesture would be read as both a welcome to his kitchen and a thank you for the man's sterling efforts on his behalf, but PC Thompson only looked for the fly Albert was apparently trying to scare off.

'How may I help you, officer?' Albert tried as the silence stretched.

'It's probably nothing, sir, but if you're sure you're all right?'

'All fine now, officer. Toast dislodged. Would you like a cup of tea?'

'Not on duty, sir,' Thompson replied, shaking his head sadly as if all the world's ills could be laid at the feet of tea.

'I have to open the shop in a minute,' Albert prompted.

Thompson nodded and, to Albert's silent horror, produced a notebook from his chest pocket.

'This is only a routine inquiry, sir, if you understand. It's just that your bank reported an unusual transaction. I was in the area and I said I'd pop in and have a chat about it. Nothing formal, Mr Rossi.'

'A banking matter?' Albert asked in surprise and relief. 'Well! They have persecuted me for some years now, PC Thompson. I am happy to give my side of the story and perhaps you'll appreciate then . . .'

'It's about the twenty thousand pounds in cash that you paid in the day before yesterday, sir, if you don't mind,' Thompson said, checking his notebook for a moment. 'I'm sure it can be explained, but when large amounts of cash are moved about, it generates a warning flag at the Organised Crime Unit, sir.' For an instant, the policeman's eyes grew wistful. 'They get all the bells and whistles, sir, money no object with them. As I say, I was just passing and I said I'd drop in and check it was all above board.'

Albert felt his eyes beginning to bulge again as his mind raced. The haunting strains of Albinoni's Adagio in G minor seemed to fill his ears, somewhere around the bit with dramatic chords. It was not a pleasant sensation.

PC Thompson waited and the silence grew longer and longer. Albert's mind was a complete blank. He couldn't say it was his savings, after almost a decade of reporting losses on the shop. He toyed with the idea of saying he had found it, but he had a suspicion that honest subjects of the Queen were meant to hand large bags of cash to the authorities, not pay their debts with them. He opened his mouth slowly, in the hope that the action would force an idea out. What would a fellow assassin say to such a question? Did they even pay income tax? He thought it was unlikely. Suddenly, an idea tickled his forebrain.

'Gambling!' Albert Rossi said in triumph. He reached into his pocket for a large linen handkerchief, shaking it out with a flourish and wiping his forehead.

'*Gambling*, sir?' PC Thompson replied. There was more than a hint of displeasure in those few words and Albert Rossi swallowed nervously.

'In a casino!' Albert added, knowing he couldn't name the winner of any horse race. Roulette was the sort of thing he expected assassins to do, though he had only ever seen it in the films. He braced himself for more questions, knowing that his future depended on how well he remembered *Ocean's Eleven*, a popular film about a casino robbery that he'd watched only for the suits. In fairness, the suits were the best bit.

'I see, sir. So you're saying you won twenty thousand pounds. In one evening, sir?'

Albert sensed the trap. For all he knew, casinos kept records of large wins.

'Oh no, I only ever play for small stakes. It was over a year or two.'

'You must have a system, sir. That's a lot of money. Roulette, was it? Punto banco? Blackjack?'

Albert wiped his forehead again. He could feel his armpits getting damp. He'd never heard of 'punto banco'. He imagined himself nodding happily and the policeman saying, 'But actually, sir, a punto banco is a small fish from the River Amazon,' or something like that. He decided to play safe.

'Roulette, mostly.'

'Sounds like a good club, sir. Which one was it again?'

PC Thompson leaned forward slightly in his seat, but Albert relaxed visibly. A few years before, he'd been caught short in London and had popped into a plush-looking establishment. He remembered the name.

'The Ingot, in Quebec Street. Lovely place – very attractive dark blue carpet.' He closed his mouth with a snap, aware that he'd gone a little too far.

'Not many men notice the carpet, sir,' PC Thompson said, frowning. To Albert's relief, he began to put his notebook away.

'I'm ... an observant man, officer,' Albert replied, trying a smile that he hoped looked more confident than he felt. He could hear a phone ringing in his bedroom, and his eyes swivelled in that direction. 'If that's all, Officer Thompson, I have to take that call.'

'Some sort of waistcoat emergency, sir?' PC Thompson said sourly. There was a hint of disappointment in his eyes.

'Could well be, officer. You never know in this game.'

The policeman rose and carefully set the chair back in its place.

'Well, I won't keep you, sir. Gambling *does* explain how you came into possession of twenty thousand pounds in used notes, yes. I'll be in touch if there's anything else.'

The policeman didn't sound satisfied, Albert noticed. There was a definite note of frost in the air as he left.

Harefield Hospital is an emergency facility on the north-western edge of London, specialising in the treatment of heart and lung ailments. Most of the patients are elderly and very often the task of the staff is simply to prevent imminent death and then send them off-site to other wards to recover from their ordeal.

John Halliday was not a normal patient in any sense. Not only was he younger than the others by about forty years, but his injuries had come from a car accident, or so the police claimed. Even they were not sure, as he had been found unconscious and badly injured on Hawthorn Avenue in Eastcote, some twelve days before. For six of those days he had hovered on the edge of death's dark doorway – holding on to the handle perhaps, but with fingers slowly slipping. Then he had surfaced for a time and sheer rage seemed to aid his recovery from that point. He had a memory of talking to a well-dressed man in the road, then a vision of a Nissan Micra coming straight at him. As soon as he was awake, he had questioned the nurses and even read his own chart with a sinking feeling. The impact had created a blood clot in an artery. As a result, he'd had a heart attack and been rushed to Harefield.

Halliday had not been a pleasant man before the heart attack. On the morning of 11 September 2001, when planes were hijacked over New York, the last communications sent by mobile phone and picked up across the world were, with one exception, heartfelt and moving messages of love. That exception had been the one left on the answering machine of John Halliday. It had come from his own brother.

'I haven't got long now,' his brother had said over the noise of roaring aero engines. 'I just wanted you to know that you . . . are a complete shit.'

Being run over and suffering a heart attack had done nothing to improve the personality of a man already capable of inspiring such dislike. He had not seen a white light or spoken to an angel. If he had, he would have punched that angel in the kidney.

According to the nurses, the police still wanted

to speak to him, though it seemed they thought of him as some sort of bizarre victim. It hadn't helped that his false teeth had been knocked out in the collision with Albert Rossi's Micra. A very young policeman had bagged them as evidence, much as an iPhone-using schoolboy might have regarded a relic from the distant past, like a codpiece, or a cassette player. Without the teeth, Halliday had experienced enormous difficulties making himself understood.

His mood had worsened still further when his dentures were finally returned. Some well-meaning soul had decided that they needed to be disinfected. Presumably they had been popped into a glass of neat bleach out of kindness, but the result was the pink plastic gums had whitened as much as the false teeth. When he smiled now, people backed away as if from a shark – perhaps even a shark in an advert for Colgate toothpaste, with real gleam.

Halliday did not understand why they hadn't found his gun, but there was no police guard sitting by his bed, and over the previous week they appeared to have forgotten about him. As it happens, Halliday did not want to speak to the police at all. He might have vanished from the medical care unit on a quiet night if they hadn't put him on a catheter. It worked a lot

31

better than handcuffs, he discovered. You can wrench and struggle against handcuffs. With practice and skill, you can even pick the lock. A tube leading straight up your penis is quite a different matter.

He resolved to wait. Someone would pay for every humiliation. They would pay for the shockingly white smile, the bed baths and the bruises. They would pay for the irritating old lady across the room who kept throwing grapes at him. They would pay for every moment of pain and weakness he had suffered. He did not yet know the name of Albert Rossi. If he had, it would have given focus to waking moments filled with the desire for revenge.

Halliday could have made a certain phone call from the bed. He was not used to the idea of subcontracting work, but a single call could set very dark forces in motion. The idea was certainly tempting. However, this was personal, perhaps a more personal debt than he had ever known before. Halliday knew about debts. Up to that point in his life, he had settled every last one of them himself.

With cheerful thoughts of murder and Micras wafting through his head, he fell asleep once more.

Chapter Five

Albert Rossi sat on a chair by his bed, sucking his finger where he had caught it trying to reload the Colt pistol. He didn't have the internet himself, but a visit to the local library had revealed that it was a semi-automatic and, though obsolete, had once been a favourite with American armed forces. He liked that. He liked everything about the gun. He found his fingers drawn to it as it lay on his paisley-patterned quilt, caressing the metal with all the attention he might have given a lover, if he'd ever had one who wasn't more interested in beefsteak and kidneys. The Colt 1911 was wonderfully impersonal. It was almost as if you could point it at someone and say 'Bang', then watch them fall over. That hadn't actually happened with Peter Schenk, but it might have done. Albert was still avoiding thinking about the consequences or even the basic reality of his new profession. The idea of, say, sticking a knife into someone would have simply horrified him.

The greasy brown envelope lay torn on the floor and the contents were spread all over his coverlet. He had begun to understand that there was both good and bad news about the life of an assassin. The good news was that honest, decent family men were not likely to become targets, at least in his limited experience so far. The file he had read could only be described as disturbing – and there were photographs in it that he never wanted to see again. The bad news was that the sort of men who did attract the notice of paid killers usually had some inkling of the dangerous life they led.

Just as Peter Schenk had employed armed guards, so this new man, Victor Stasiak, had entrusted his safety to two ferocious dogs – *and* armed guards. Running him over was not a serious prospect and sadly the man had no passion for hang-gliding. As Albert read through the file, he noted a long-term interest in photography, but the potential for violent, sudden death seemed limited there.

Whoever had the task of researching the targets had done an incredibly thorough job, that much was obvious. As well as three different addresses around London and one in the Lake District,

Albert had all the details he could possibly need. The house in Cumbria looked the most promising, if only because it was isolated and less likely to attract the attention of half a million Metropolitan policemen, among them one PC George Thompson, with his unpleasant interest in used notes and bank accounts.

Albert had even *negotiated*, when the voice called back to confirm he had received the envelope. In Albert's experience, negotiation was an achingly embarrassing thing. He had once offered 80 per cent of the price for his washing machine, only to be told that Comet was a bit different to Wembley Market. In Wembley Market, he had offered half the asking price for a bottle of shampoo, but they said it was full price or he could push off. They hadn't said 'push', either. One of his least favourite memories was having a kitchen installed three years before. Whenever he made the builders a cup of tea, the price had mysteriously gone up. In the end, he had spent the night in the Tudor Lodge Hotel rather than bankrupt himself with yet another conversation.

In his new persona as killer-for-hire, he had assumed a gruff voice and told his caller he wanted double the usual fee. To his amazement and delight, the voice had agreed, just like that. Twenty thousand pounds was a lot of money, by almost anyone's standards. It would clear Albert's debt to the bank and might even leave enough over for a trip to a casino. Albert stroked the pistol as he considered getting out of the life after that. He'd been lucky, but it couldn't go on. One last job and he would be done with death, he told himself. He'd keep the gun, obviously, for home defence, or as a memento. He smiled wryly as the memory of an old Latin lesson came back to him: a *memento mori* – a reminder of death.

He made his plans that night and the following morning left a note on the shop door that said he would be closed for a few days. Experience suggested that not too many Eastcote residents would be disappointed by that, but it was basic good manners. He walked past the butcher's shop on the way home and could not help glowering through the window.

The Nissan Micra 1.2 is quite a small car and his particular problem was that he didn't know exactly what equipment he would need to gain entrance to a mansion in Cumbria. Albert had access to a small garage below the flats and over the years he had filled it with the same things as most other people. An ancient canvas rucksack caught his eye. Metal bowls and a tin cup clanked inside from some old camping trip. On a shelf, he found a roll of duct tape – Albert was perhaps the only man in England who pronounced the 't', instead of referring to it as 'duck' tape. He spent a long time looking at a pair of pliers before putting them back with a sigh. A hammer seemed generally useful and he found a roll of rope that he had bought as a makeshift washing line years before. His best find was a pair of ancient binoculars, looking as if they had last been used to search for German battleships in the Channel.

A very old tool roll was helpful in putting his little kit together and at last the Micra was loaded and ready to go. According to his *AA Road Atlas*, Cumbria was just shy of three hundred miles away. As he drove through Ickenham towards the motorways that would take him north, he worked out his journey times in calm anticipation. Victor Stasiak did not know it, but death was heading up the M1 towards him.

When it isn't raining, Cumbria is ranked among the most beautiful parts of England. It is difficult to confirm this because it's always, *always* raining. The inhabitants delight and frolic in it, telling themselves that at least gardeners will be pleased. Gardeners are sometimes washed away in Cumbria. It has mountains as well, however, so those gentlemen are rarely washed far. They usually end up in a gully of some kind.

Albert had an umbrella, of course. It was a beautiful thing, bought from James Smith and Sons on New Oxford Street. It had struts and spars and it hummed in the wind as he heaved it open into a wet Cumbrian gale. He had also chosen a tweed jacket, expecting it to help him blend in up north. It is a little-known fact that one stage of making tweed cloth involves leaving it to soak in urine. Sheep urine is much prized but for obvious reasons is extremely difficult to collect. They won't stand still. Human urine is the only remaining choice, and as a result there was a faint odour of wee around Albert as his jacket grew damp.

He had parked his car in a town his map told him was called Keswick and was walking down a rainy street where every second shop sold waterproof clothing and hiking boots. Or heavy jumpers. Or old-fashioned sweets, for some reason. Perhaps hikers take comfort in barley twists or lemon drops as they wait for the rain to stop. It never does, though, so some of them never come down.

Albert had a huge choice of places offering bed and breakfast, down every side street. He picked one at random and lugged his heavy bag and umbrella through the door. He told himself wearily that tomorrow would do well enough to despatch Victor Stasiak from this world to the next.

Chapter Six

Halliday stood outside the main entrance to Harefield Hospital, shivering slightly in a grey drizzle. He was out. More importantly, the catheter was out. He was free. He had made a call at last from inside the hospital and a long, black car was now sliding through the rain towards him, parking itself on a set of red lines usually reserved for ambulances. He opened the door, wincing slightly as the stitches in his groin pulled with the motion. It was a mystery to him why the doctors had decided to approach his heart from as far away as a vein in his leg. Perhaps they enjoyed the challenge.

From his chart he had learned that a tiny cage had been inserted in his heart, a 'stent', as they called it. It held the vein open and allowed the blood clot to disperse. He frowned at the thought of the strange thing keeping him alive. Presumably they knew their business. He was walking again, after all. He set his jaw as he slid into the back seat of the car and nodded to the driver. He knew his business as well. In ten years of successful work, he had not suffered a single injury or come close to talking to a policeman – until a complete stranger had run him over in a side street with a Nissan Micra. It was frankly humiliating, but he knew how to handle problems like that.

'I need another gun,' he growled.

The driver nodded and opened the glove compartment, handing back an oiled Colt Government and two clips of ammunition. Halliday tested the mechanism with swift, much-practised moves before showing his teeth in a savage smile. The driver blinked into the mirror at the white glare, but wisely decided not to notice.

'Where to?' the driver said.

Halliday didn't have to think. He'd had time to plan in the endless days in the ward.

'Eastcote. The Tudor Lodge Hotel.'

It would do as a base for a few days while he found out everything he needed to know. He didn't like to admit it, but he also needed more time to recover. His heart had been damaged while part of it was blocked shut. The slightest exertion set off sharp pains across his chest and made him gasp as if he'd been running a fast mile. Although he hated the idea, Halliday was forced to admit it might be time to collect his savings and retire. There was just one last job to do first.

As the limousine pulled away from the hospital, they passed a lone police car coming the other way. Both of the uniformed occupants looked over at the black car, but they couldn't see through the darkened windows. John Halliday smiled to himself. He had nothing to fear from their questions now. He hadn't given them his real name and they could search for 'Nigel Farnsley' all they wanted. He gripped the pistol tightly, taking comfort from the familiar weight. Someone was *definitely* going to pay for what had been done to him.

Albert's first problem after breakfast was confirming that Victor Stasiak was in residence. A man with at least three houses – the ones Albert knew about – could not be pinned down easily in one spot. Albert had brought enough money for a week at the bed and breakfast. If that failed, he knew he would have to try his luck in London. That was not a pleasant prospect. London was full of potential witnesses and there was something about the empty ruggedness of Cumbria that appealed to the assassin in him.

As a boy, he had read *The Thirty-Nine Steps* by John Buchan, which involved gentlemen wearing tweed chasing other, more unsavoury, gentlemen across the moors of Scotland. He could not recall all the details, but in his hiking gear, with the wind, and of course the rain, he felt glorious. In waterproof Gore-Tex trousers, with a rucksack and a large map flapping in the wind, he might as well have been invisible as he trudged up hill and down dale – and sometimes up dale and down hill. There were a few others like him, hardy-looking men for the most part, out enjoying the rain and the cold. For Cumbria, it was a fine morning.

Keswick town lies on the edge of a huge lake named Derwentwater. Albert hadn't wanted to park too close to his quarry, but as the morning wore on, he found he'd underestimated the distances involved. At first, he took long, deep breaths and strode along the edge of the lake. By the time he'd worked his way through the valley of Borrowdale, he was weary. He slogged through Honister Pass and began the long ascent of the fell known as Rannerdale Knotts. It looked over the lakes of Buttermere and Crummock Water, and as he read each name on the map,

Albert Rossi began to wonder if he'd somehow wandered into the set of *The Hobbit*.

He reached the summit by the early afternoon, fairly close to exhaustion. Only the sight of Buttermere village below raised his spirits. Victor Stasiak had his holiday home there and it was high summer, when the rain warms a bit. Albert stood panting, chewing on something called Kendal Mint Cake, which seemed to be a kind of brittle glass made of sugar. He worked a piece out from where it had impaled the roof of his mouth and stood looking down on the houses below. It was a little depressing to see a nice road running close by. Clearly he could have spared himself the hike, but his aim of scouting the area from a safe distance had certainly been fulfilled. Albert could feel the weight of the pistol in his rucksack. It could also have been his flask, or the paperback book he had brought with him, or the binoculars, or even the bulky file with all the vital details of Victor Stasiak's life, but in his imagination, it was definitely the gun.

Victor Stasiak was excited. An observer would have seen no betraying sparkle in his eyes as he flipped and tugged his tie into a Windsor knot, gazing into a long mirror as he did so. The face that looked back was heavy-jowled and serious, with a solid jaw almost submerged in the layers of good living. Freshly shaved and gleaming rolls of pink fat disappeared into his collar. If the same observer was feeling unkind, he might have described it as the face of an elderly carp, with thicker lips than are usual on a man. When Victor Stasiak tensed his jaw, the lower lip overrode the top one. A determined carp then, a carp who has met most of life's little irritations and triumphed over them. A carp, in fact, who tended to leave life's little irritations in graves around the Cumbrian countryside.

Victor Stasiak cared nothing for scenic beauty. His entire purpose in choosing a holiday home close by Buttermere lake was its suitability for burying his competitors. Let's assume for a moment that they were at least dead first. It wasn't always true, but let's assume it anyway.

With a soft grunt, Victor Stasiak finished with his tie and held out his arms for a long cashmere coat that would have caught Albert Rossi's interest immediately. His manservant raised it at the right moment, so that the fleshy arms vanished into the long sleeves and short-fingered, heavy hands poked out at the other end. It was a good coat and proof against the worst Cumbrian weather.

Yet such things were wasted on the man they

contained. The reason for Victor Stasiak's excitement lay not with the prospect of an invigorating walk, or even the finest of cashmere. He was looking forward to meeting his second in command in one of the most scenic spots in Buttermere. He was looking forward to it because he had discovered the man had been cheating him over a number of years.

Victor Stasiak smiled at his reflection. A contented carp looked back. He had chosen the spot carefully, a bridge over the longest waterfall in Cumbria. He would enjoy seeing his colleague falling onto the rocks below.

It was a rare event for Victor Stasiak to get his own hands dirty with such things, but the betrayal was a personal thing for him. He smiled again. A personal personnel issue. To be able to make a pun, even a weak one, in English was a source of some pride for him. He flexed his hands, imagining them around a throat. It would be a good day.

'Bring the car round to the front,' he told his servant. 'Have Jonas and Walker follow me in the Audi with the dogs.'

'Yes, sir,' his manservant said, bowing low.

It took time to train his staff to the right level of obedience, but Victor Stasiak believed it was worthwhile. For a man who had grown up in the steelyards of a Lithuanian port, such things were a simple joy.

'Hat,' Victor Stasiak said.

A heavy black bowler was held out and he fitted it carefully onto the dome of a head almost as perfectly round as the hat itself. Victor Stasiak was not a fool. He knew the English bowler hat had not been in fashion for sixty years or more. As a younger man, he had been impressed by a Bond film, in which the villain wore such a hat, complete with a metal rim capable of decapitating statues. Victor Stasiak had never thrown his hat at anyone, but the idea of a razor-sharp ring of steel available to him when all else failed was very much in keeping with his character. In addition, it suited him.

As well as the smell of wet tweed, which gives the House of Lords its distinctive odour, it is another little-known fact that Britain has the most extensive network of number-plate-recognition cameras in the world. Most motorways, main roads and town centres are covered by it. The information is kept for up to five years and a policeman with an interest in a particular vehicle could, if he so chose, call up video records of its travels over that entire period.

PC George Thompson was well aware of the

irritating criminal tendency to swap their own number plates for those of a tractor, or just an innocent car of the same make. Every year, tractor owners in particular were forced to contact the Metropolitan Police and point out that while they would *love* to have been doing a hundred miles an hour in London, it simply wasn't possible in a Massey Ferguson. He doubted Albert Rossi had gone to those lengths to avoid detection and he was not disappointed.

Thompson sipped at a cup of dark orange tea and tapped idly at a computer in Uxbridge police station. It was six o'clock in the morning and he had come in early to gain access to a computer that usually took eleven close-written forms even to touch. He had found the password jotted down in the desk drawer and if anyone checked, the records would show his absent colleague had become fascinated by a particular Nissan Micra. George Thompson looked grim as he sipped and tapped and then worked the mouse for a bit.

He could not have explained his suspicions about Albert Rossi. The sudden appearance of cash was certainly interesting; so were the weak excuses Rossi had offered to explain his good fortune. Fishing brown envelopes out of station bins was another black mark against him. Yet there was something more; Thompson could *feel* it. He was a believer in instinct and when his return visit had found the shop closed and Albert Rossi apparently vanished, his instincts had stopped gently prodding and begun a more determined assault. As he sat in the office and followed the video record into Cumbria, Thompson's suspicions picked up a cricket bat and looked meaningfully at him.

Something was up. He was aware that he didn't have a shred of real evidence. His superiors were unlikely to fund a day away from his desk on nothing more than a series of hunches. Yet he had a week of leave to use up and there were worse ways to spend it. He made up his mind. His Rover 75 could put him in Cumbria by noon at the latest. Where was the last hit from the cameras? He checked again and nodded to himself. Four miles outside Keswick, a traffic camera had recorded the little Micra buzzing its way north. Keswick. Thompson knocked back the last of the tea. At worst, he would have a half-day by a pleasant lake, but it was just possible that he would also discover what the *hell* was going on.

Chapter Seven

Albert Rossi approached the house he had marked on his map, creeping down a hillside in darting movements as he passed from tree to tree. He reached the bottom, hidden behind an enormous privet hedge that ran the length of the drive, at almost exactly the moment two black cars swung round to the front door. As Albert watched, the rear one was loaded with burly men and two snarling Alsatian dogs. He sank lower into old vegetation, suddenly terrified that he would be seen.

He hardly needed his binoculars. Twenty yards from him, the front door opened and Victor Stasiak came out, sheltered from the rain by another man carrying an umbrella. Albert felt his pulse race at the sight of his quarry. The tendency to wear black bowlers had been mentioned in the file but even if Stasiak had been bare-headed, there was no mistaking the heavy frame. The coat was very good quality, Albert noted, a little enviously. It seemed crime paid rather well.

The experience with hang-gliding and Peter Schenk had not prepared him for the sheer excitement of a hunter facing a dangerous enemy. Or at least, looking at him from under a hedge. Albert Rossi's heart pounded wildly and his hands shook as he took hold of the pistol, more for comfort than anything. It was heady stuff for the owner of a men's clothing shop.

The thrill lasted just long enough for Victor Stasiak to climb into the back seat of the first car, a huge Mercedes. The car door was shut by his manservant and in just a few seconds both vehicles purred their way past Albert Rossi in the undergrowth, down the long drive and were gone. The gates closed slowly on unseen motors. Albert tutted to himself, but he was not disappointed. At the very least, he had confirmed Stasiak was in Cumbria. He watched as the house became quiet once more.

An experienced assassin would probably not have done what Albert Rossi decided to do next. The more professional members of that deadly craft have learned the hard way to make plans and stick with them. They have also learned not to commit small crimes that could get them caught in possession of the tools of their trade. They do not speed on motorways and they park carefully. Perhaps above all else, they do not steal a postman's bike when it is left within twenty feet of them by a cheerful Cumbrian.

Albert watched as the gates to the estate opened once more. His gaze flicked to the red and black bicycle leaning against the hedge, then to the grey-haired man whistling as he approached the main house with his letters. Albert Rossi did not remember making an actual decision, but he was out of that hedge in a flurry of leaves, onto the bike and pedalling furiously through the gates before his brain caught up.

As he turned into the road, heading in the same direction as the black cars, Albert wobbled out of control. Most men assume they will be able to ride a bike for ever. There is even a phrase – 'like riding a bike' – that indicates it's a skill you never lose once you have gained it. The truth is that childhood skill does not always equal middle-aged skill and Albert very nearly crashed into a tractor on the first bend. Admittedly, the driver of the tractor was distracted as he considered how to reply to a letter accusing him of doing eighty miles an hour in Piccadilly. That combination of distraction, mild rain and lack of skill very nearly ended the career and the life of Albert Rossi. After a moment of flashing images, he found himself in a second hedge, scratched and red-faced, as the tractor driver shouted something unprintable and went on, feeling much better about his own troubles.

Flushed and sweating, Albert pulled himself out and resumed the chase. He was still working on instinct and he peered ahead at every turn of the road for a glimpse of black cars.

Life is full of small choices that can have large effects. If President Lincoln had chosen to stay at home rather than go to the theatre, much of history would be very different. If Victor Stasiak hadn't decided to send one of his men running into a corner shop in Buttermere village to buy a cigar, Albert would have been unlikely to catch up with them.

Puffing wearily, with his legs already aching, he stopped at the edge of the village and was rewarded by the sight of the two cars waiting at a kerb with engines running. With a huge effort, he steadied his breathing. The gun was back in his rucksack and his prey was in sight. He could only hope Victor Stasiak wasn't heading towards the motorway. Albert Rossi had visions of the bikeless postman calling the police and fresh beads of sweat broke out on his forehead. If the local constabulary spotted him, he would surely be searched. The gun would be found.

Realising his danger, Albert stepped off the postman's bike, but as he leaned it against a fence, Stasiak's cars moved off with a low growl. Albert made a similar sound in the back of his throat. Visions of twenty thousand pounds and freedom from the bank floated across his imagination. He leapt back on, keeping his head down as he pedalled after them, heading through the village and out into the open countryside.

Victor Stasiak climbed slowly out of the car, without bothering to acknowledge the bodyguard holding the door and an umbrella. He could hear the roar of the waterfall nearby, but, as was often the case in Cumbria, he would have to walk the last part to get up to the bridge that crossed its highest point.

The rain was particularly heavy that day, but even so there were one or two families and hikers trudging up the hill. Victor frowned at the sight of them. It was a few minutes to noon and he needed privacy to carry out the unpleasant business he had planned. As he stood there, another black car crunched to a halt on the broken ground and his best friend for thirty years got out.

Auguste Nerius was a thin man, wiry and still black-haired despite his age. Victor suspected he dyed it, but he had never asked. Nerius had been with Victor in the shipyards, running a small stolen-car ring and a betting consortium. When the authorities had finally closed in on them, they had taken ship to the United Kingdom, just two more immigrants with a bagful of used notes. The seed money had given them something of a jump start and their shipping contacts meant they could import almost anything. They had got in at the beginning of a massive cocaine market in the seventies and made several fortunes.

Victor greeted his oldest friend with a broad smile and patted him on the back.

'Let's walk,' he said, without explanation.

As always, he was impossible to refuse and Nerius merely shrugged and followed. He had always been the planner, a man of few words, while Victor was the one who met clients and impressed them with his ruthlessness and charisma. It had been a good partnership. As they turned together to walk up the path, Victor shook his head in sadness. Some men are never satisfied, no matter how much they own. Nerius had been like a brother to him, but that made the betrayal all the more painful – and the anger more fierce.

Neither man took any notice of the middle-aged cyclist who leaned his bike against a tree and stood with his hands on his knees, gasping and red-faced. After a time, Albert lay down on his back and wheezed at the grey clouds overhead. Victor Stasiak's bodyguards stared at him as they brought the dogs out of the second car and let them sniff around on short leashes, but there was nothing about Albert Rossi to arouse suspicion, unless perhaps you worked for the Post Office and recognised the bike. Victor and Nerius led the way and the bodyguards followed. The small group left Albert behind as they strolled along the winding track that would take them across the very top of the waterfall.

Chapter Eight

Victor Stasiak was beginning to regret his taste for the dramatic. He suspected he should have taken Nerius somewhere quiet and simply put a bullet in his head. His bodyguards were good with shovels and Cumbria is almost designed for the easy disposal of dead colleagues, with hidden valleys and clefts by the hundred. Yet for his oldest friend, Victor had imagined a grand finale, a few last words, then a silent fall onto the smooth black boulders far below. He had not imagined a child licking an ice cream and watching them both with dull fascination, nor the two mums walking a squalling baby back and forth across the bridge. In his imagination, the bridge over the waterfall had been deserted and windswept. He frowned to himself. Nerius was still waiting for whatever was so important that his boss and friend had to summon him to such an odd place.

Victor looked at him and drummed his fingers on the wooden railing of the bridge.

'Did the latest shipment come in all right?' he said at last.

Nerius shrugged and nodded. Britain was that wonderful combination of an island and a trading nation, so that ships came and went twenty-four hours a day. It really wasn't difficult to get a small, high-value item like cocaine into one of the great ports. With the best will in the world, the customs officers couldn't search every container. Victor usually left that side of things to Nerius, while he set up the meetings and links in the chain further down.

The girl with the ice cream stepped closer to stare at the two men talking in a strange language. Victor glowered at her, without making the slightest impression. He had been intending to confront Nerius with his knowledge, see the awareness of real danger creep into the man's face, then pitch him over the railing. He couldn't really raise the subject with the prospect of having to wait another half an hour for the bridge to clear. Yet Nerius was growing suspicious, he could sense it. He needed a topic to pass the time. Inspiration struck him and Victor Stasiak relaxed.

'I'm thinking of retiring, Nerius, old friend,' he said. 'I've made my money and I'm not a young man any more.'

Nerius looked sharply at him, searching his face with his eyes. The two mums had finally rocked the baby to sleep and one of them was calling for the little girl to come with them. Victor nodded to himself. His bodyguards were further down the track, trying hard to look as if they were just out walking two savage Alsatians.

'We've . . . um . . . we've had some good times,' Victor went on vaguely.

The little girl wandered off, looking back at them with every step as she followed the two mums. For the first time, the bridge was empty. As he tensed for action Victor saw what looked like a Scout troop rounding the closest bend, led by a bearded man in shorts.

'Oh, for God's *sake* . . .' Victor Stasiak said. 'There's no privacy here.'

In moments, the bridge filled with boys peering over the edge while their harassed scoutmaster warned them constantly that they would fall if they leant that far out. Victor tried not to listen, but he learned more about that bridge and water-fall in the next minute than he had ever wanted to know.

To his surprise, Nerius suddenly spoke, the

words hoarse from a man who weighed them like gold and spent them only rarely.

'I am . . . pleased to hear that. I can take over, Victor. We can work something out.'

Victor Stasiak blinked at him in surprise. He opened his mouth to reply, but the scoutmaster was already pointing further down the hill. The group began to move away. Swiftly, Victor checked both directions, seeing only the backs of young Scouts hurrying to catch up with the rest. He failed to see Albert Rossi brace himself against a tree some way off the path. Albert was muddy and exhausted from scrambling over rough ground, but at last he was close enough to bring his gun to bear on the two men.

'I would have liked that, Nerius,' Victor Stasiak went on. 'Yes, I can say it to you now. I would have liked you to take over, after me. I have no sons, Nerius. You would have made me proud.' He checked the paths again. Finally they were alone.

A hundred yards away, Albert Rossi wiped sweat from his eyes and rested the long silencer on a small branch, squinting along it.

'There is only one small problem, old friend,' Victor said.

Nerius raised his eyebrows in silent enquiry.

'Small dogs should not show their teeth to big dogs, Nerius. When they do, they get hurt.'

'What do you mean?' Nerius asked in genuine confusion.

'I mean you should have told me about the shipment from the Ukraine, old friend. It should have turned up on the books and it did not. Did you really think I wouldn't find out about you stealing from me?'

Nerius understood suddenly that he was very alone. He stepped away from Victor Stasiak and his muscles tensed to run. In doing so, he gave Albert Rossi a perfect, clear shot.

With a grim expression, Albert squeezed the trigger, then squeezed it again, much harder, so that his hand shook with the effort.

'Safety catch!' he whispered to himself, flicking it across with his finger and resuming his position, squinting along the barrel.

His mouth fell open in surprise. In that brief moment of inattention, the situation on the bridge had changed dramatically.

Victor Stasiak had Nerius by the throat. The smaller man was struggling violently, hammering at the hands that held him. They staggered left, then right as Albert Rossi looked on in astonishment. It seemed almost rude to interrupt his kill in such a way, as if they were not taking him seriously at all.

The wooden bridge across the waterfall was

well built and solid. It was quite capable of preventing Boy Scouts from falling to their deaths, with a little care. It was not, however, capable of withstanding the sixteen stone of Victor Stasiak, combined with the twelve stone of Auguste Nerius, suddenly slamming against the railing. It gave way and both men flailed in horror as they plunged over the edge and tumbled to the rocks far below. For reasons Albert did not understand, Victor Stasiak's spinning bowler hat landed on the wooden bridge and stuck there, quivering.

For the second time in his brief career as an assassin, Albert Rossi watched men fall to their deaths. He was obscurely disappointed. He'd been looking forward to using the gun and if it hadn't been for the rotten safety catch, he'd . . . He caught himself, realising lots of different things at once. He would be paid a small fortune, for a start. Victor Stasiak was definitely dead and that meant he'd succeeded, at least as far as Stephen Hawking was concerned.

More pressing, though, was the sudden shouting of bodyguards nearby, combined with the barking of dogs. Albert Rossi was fairly certain they would see that a terrible accident had occurred. However, he suspected the sight of an armed man wrapped around a nearby tree might make even a simple-minded bodyguard a little suspicious. He could hear Alsatians barking furiously as the bodyguards came sprinting up to the bridge. Instinct alone made him toss the pistol into the river far below before standing up and trying very hard to look like any other hiker who happened to be wandering past.

Albert Rossi reached the bridge at the same time as the bodyguards. The Alsatian dogs growled and lunged on their short leashes, their black eyes frightening. One of the men was already gesturing wildly, speaking into a mobile phone in a language Albert couldn't understand.

Albert felt it would be suspicious to ignore the scene, so he sidled close to the broken rail like any other interested passer-by. He was looking at the sprawled bodies far below when one of the guards grabbed him by the scruff of the neck.

'You . . . go! Go away now!' the man said, gesturing down the path.

With a frown at the man's bad manners, Albert did as he was told, trying not to let them see how his legs were shaking. That was it, he told himself. That was the last job he'd take. He could still recall the moment of puzzled terror as Victor Stasiak caught sight of him in mid-fall. The look in the man's eyes had been an awful thing to witness and Albert shuddered as he reached the bottom of the track.

To his surprise, there was a policeman standing by the postman's bicycle, but Albert had been dealing with worse things than that and he strolled on, passing the police car parked nearby. He was close enough to hear the radio splutter as the message came in about a Boy Scout troop who had been splashing around in the pools below only to have two men bounce off the rocks around them. That was a trip they wouldn't forget, Albert Rossi thought with a smile. He wondered if there was a badge for that.

As he made it back to the road, he realised he didn't regret the decision he had made. Albert Rossi was cut out for a lot of things, but the life of an assassin was too noisy, too fraught with danger and, frankly, too stressful. He almost looked forward to quiet days back in the shop, or he could even retire.

A thought struck him. He owed himself a visit to a casino first. He began to whistle, walking along a leafy lane towards Buttermere.

Chapter Nine

PC George Thompson almost choked on his lemonade when he saw Albert Rossi again. For a moment, he thought there would be a nasty repeat of their first meeting, but this time with Rossi thumping *him* on the back. He had been sitting at a table under a café awning, coincidentally close to the Nissan Micra he had followed north, when the man himself strolled by, whistling to himself as if he didn't have a care in the world.

As a general rule, policemen don't enjoy the sight of cheerful, carefree people and PC Thompson was no exception. He finished coughing out the last gulp of lemonade he'd inhaled and stood up suddenly to bar Albert Rossi's path. They faced each other in mutual suspicion and surprise.

For the first few moments, Albert could not reconcile the face of the policeman with his recent experiences. In Albert's mind, the policeman had a definite context and a café in Cumbria was not it. For his part, PC George Thompson could hardly believe how bedraggled and muddy Albert Rossi was. He looked as if he'd leapt through a hedge, hiked over a mountain and slid down a hill until a tree arrested his descent.

All of that was in fact true. It had been a busy morning for Albert Rossi. Mud-spattered and weary though he was, he was also feeling very pleased with himself. He recognised the moustache and smiled.

'Afternoon, George,' Albert said cheerily. 'Or I suppose it's evening by now. I didn't expect to see the long arm of the law so far out of London.'

PC Thompson narrowed his eyes at this casual use of his first name.

'I'm on leave for a couple of days,' he said grimly. 'Might I ask your reason for suddenly visiting the Lake District?' He remembered Rossi as a nervous little man, not this breezy fellow in hiking gear with a mischievous expression.

Albert Rossi was in the pleasant situation of knowing he had committed no crime barring the theft of a bicycle. Oh, he had *intended* terrible dark deeds, no doubt about it, but as it happens, none of them had actually come off. He didn't even have the gun any longer. All in all, it had been a lovely holiday and he couldn't resist tweaking the nose of a policeman who had lost his power to intimidate.

'Just getting away from the smog, George, don't you know? Bit of fresh air, hiking in the rain, seeing God's creatures up close – that sort of thing.'

'I see. So it wouldn't have anything to do with a large amount of money in used notes then?'

It was, admittedly, a stab in the dark to see what reaction he would get. Albert Rossi only chuckled and tutted in gentle reproof.

'No casinos around here, George. Just hills and . . . waterfalls and things. Beautiful. You should try it a bit, before you go back. Now, lovely to see you, but I've a long drive ahead.'

Albert Rossi even considered patting the policeman on the shoulder, though in the end he thought that might be a step too far. He felt PC Thompson's stare between his shoulder blades as he reached his car and dumped the rucksack into the boot. Perhaps he can be excused the cheery wave he gave the policeman before settling himself in and tuning the radio to his favourite station.

Bonnie Tyler began to build towards a powerful chorus and Albert grinned to himself, put the car in gear and went home.

A week later, Albert took some of the money he had been paid and walked it through the polished doors of the Ingot in Quebec Street, London. He stood in the entrance and breathed in the atmosphere: the dark tables, the quiet hum of talk, the click of chips and the tinkle of ice in glasses. He was wearing a rather nice dinner jacket and he'd worried it would be too much in London, but he was able to relax when he saw how smartly dressed the other patrons were. As he changed a thick wad of cash for chips, he wondered how many of them were assassins enjoying the fruits of their labours. Probably not more than half a dozen at most, he thought.

By the time he came out, some six hours later, darkness had fallen in London. Albert took out a large linen handkerchief and wiped his forehead as he stood in the discreet light from the club. It had been an extraordinary evening. He felt wrung out, as if he had lived a year in just a few frantic hours. He could feel damp patches under his armpits, despite the double-strength antiperspirant he had put on earlier. He had won! For one golden evening, the gods had looked down on Albert Rossi and actually smiled. He had never had an evening like it.

In the beginning, he had put a hundred pounds on black and doubled his money. It was meant to be his farewell to the life, the insane bet that would be his final two-fingered gesture to NatWest and their letters, to all bad men and assassins everywhere. Flushed with that success, he had picked a number at random and put two blood-red chips on it. To his amazement, the croupier had pushed a big pile of chips over to him just moments later.

It is perhaps not too surprising that Albert Rossi went a little wild at that point. He'd bet on the low eighteen numbers, he'd bet on the high. He'd bet on odd numbers, then the double zero. To his delight, a crowd had gathered around him and at the peak of it all he'd even had the experience of seeing the croupier check with the floor boss.

The floor boss had looked at Albert Rossi. A slight smile had crooked the side of his mouth. Perhaps he saw only the owner of a gentleman's clothing shop in the Ingot that evening. Yet for those few, glorious hours, Albert was a little more than that. He was an assassin – retired. And he won again, after the floor boss nodded to let the stakes ride.

They brought him drinks and a plate of canapés that he wolfed down, as he hadn't eaten since lunch. He nodded to the croupier to put a thousand on number seven while he was still chewing on an avocado and prawn delight – and it came in, the perfect silver ball answering every one of his prayers. He had felt drunk on the magic of it all. Finally, the universe had given up treading on Albert Rossi. He only wished the manager of his local NatWest branch could be there to witness his triumph. The man would bite through his own hat in frustration, Albert was sure of it.

In the end, Albert pushed a tower of chips onto the square for black and watched as the silver ball bounced around, clicking and spinning. Somehow, he *knew* his luck had run out long before it came to rest in a red slot. A sigh went around the group who had gathered to watch. They looked at Albert hungrily, their eyes gleaming as they stared at the remaining stacks of chips by his right hand. Every one of them was well dressed, but for the first time in his adult life, Albert was immune to such things. There was a moment of silence as they waited for him to ride the loss and risk it all.

If he had been nothing more than a man who sold coats and socks, he might have been taken in by the false friends on all sides. Yet Albert

Rossi had stared death in the face, mostly as it was plummeting past him. With a quiet sigh, he had stood up, stepped back and asked to have his remaining chips cashed in.

Outside, a light drizzle began that couldn't even begin to dampen his mood. Despite that final loss, he had a thick bundle of notes in every pocket of his jacket and coat. He shook his head in quiet disbelief, staring at his hands in the rain as if the magic they had contained might still be seen. Somehow, he knew it had gone and gone for ever. It was a last gift and he would retire with it.

The road outside the casino was still busy at that time of night. Umbrellas hid the faces of passers-by and Albert jumped when one of them stepped in close to him without warning. He looked down at a Colt Government pistol complete with sinister black silencer. Albert gaped at the weapon, then looked slowly up into the face of the man carrying it. It was the first time he had actually seen the flinty features of John Halliday and there was nothing to reassure him there.

'We meet again, Albert,' Halliday growled at him. 'Though this time you have no car handy to run me over.'

Albert was already wearing a 'surprised spaniel'

sort of expression. As the new information sank in, it became, by degrees, 'spaniel found next to a chewed slipper'. The dazed happiness drained slowly away, leaving him feeling dizzy and slightly ill. Memories flashed at him and he made a soft, moaning sound. Was it good manners to congratulate a man on being alive when you were the one who had run him over? Albert had no idea.

'That was an accident,' he said, spluttering.

'Oh, I could have *believed* that,' Halliday said, leaning still closer and sticking the gun into Albert's midriff. 'One look at you and the words "clumsy, careless *bastard*" spring to mind. But there's more, isn't there? I made contact with my employers and do you know what they said? Do you know what they *told* me?'

His voice had risen and a few passers-by glanced over at the pair of men standing against a wall. One of them raised his eyebrows for a moment before hurrying on, but that's all you get in London, even if you run down a road naked.

Albert sighed. 'They told you I'd been carrying on with your jobs.' A faint hint of rebellion came into his tone, surprising them both. 'Pretty well, too, as it happens.'

Halliday responded by jamming the gun further into Albert's stomach, making him wince.

'They did say that, yes. But they do not appreciate sporting amateurs in this game, Albert. I hardly had to mention it before they employed me to *sort* this little problem right out!'

'I have money on me,' Albert said, looking into Halliday's insane eyes. 'Enough to pay you back for the jobs I did. You could just take it and go; no one would ever know. I'm finished anyway.'

'That's a very decent offer, Mr Rossi. A month ago, I might have accepted a nice offer like that.' Halliday smiled, which revealed a white glare of teeth and bleached gums that made Albert blink. 'However, there is the little matter of evening up the scales, Albert. I believe in scales, you see, in balance. When a man runs me over, causing me a ruptured spleen and a heart attack, there has to be justice. Do you understand? I'm not here for the money. I'm not even here to make a point about bleeding amateurs. I'm here for *justice.*'

Now that Albert was looking for it, he saw that Halliday was not in fact in the best of health. The assassin looked very pale and beads of sweat stood out on his forehead. Halliday swayed as he stood there and he kept blinking as if he was having trouble keeping Albert Rossi in focus. For the first time, Albert thought about shoving the man away and trying to make a run for it.

What happened next happened very quickly indeed. Out of the crowd, a burly figure stepped up suddenly and dropped a heavy hand onto John Halliday's shoulder.

'*Right!* Whatever's going on, I'm getting to the bottom of it *right now*. You're both *nicked*!'

It was perhaps the wrong thing to do to a man who had released himself too early from a heart ward. There was a dull thump and Halliday collapsed in a sprawl. PC George Thompson saw the gun for the first time as it clattered onto the pavement. His jaw dropped open and as he looked up he saw a wisp of smoke from a hole in Albert Rossi's jacket. Their eyes met and, without a word, Albert folded on top of Halliday.

'Bloody *hell*,' PC Thompson said to himself, in awed wonder.

He had chosen to wear plain clothes to follow Albert Rossi, but he reached into his textured polyester coat and removed a police radio, snapping out the details of the incident over the crackle of static. In the middle of London, paramedics and police would be only a minute or two away, but PC Thompson knelt and took Halliday's pulse anyway. The man was dead, his false teeth halfway out of his mouth. PC Thompson stared at them in confusion. Sharks weren't in it.

When he reached Albert Rossi, he patted the man's cheek and took his wrist, but with a sudden gasp Albert pulled it away and sat up, shaking his head groggily. His gaze took in the crouching policeman looking as if he'd seen a ghost, as well as the dead body lying next to him.

Slowly, with shaking hands, Albert Rossi opened his coat and pulled out a bundle of banknotes, tied with a gold band. His eyes widened as he saw a hole all the way through them, then he reached further to another bundle in his jacket breast pocket. There was a hole in that bundle as well, but there was also a slightly misshapen bullet.

'Bloody *hell*!' PC Thompson said again. 'Better than body armour.'

'I think you did me a bit of a favour there, George,' Albert said weakly.

Quick Reads 📖

Fall in love with reading

Doctor Who
Magic of the Angels

Jacqueline Rayner

BBC Books

'No one from this time
will ever see that girl again ...'

On a sight-seeing tour of London the Doctor wonders why so many young girls are going missing. When he sees Sammy Star's amazing magic act, he thinks he knows the answer. The Doctor and his friends team up with residents of an old people's home to discover the truth. And together they find themselves face to face with a deadly Weeping Angel.

Whatever you do – don't blink!

A thrilling all-new adventure featuring the Doctor, Amy and Rory, as played by Matt Smith, Karen Gillan and Arthur Darvill in the hit series from BBC Television.

Quick Reads

Fall in love with reading

The Little One

Lynda La Plante

Simon & Schuster

Are you scared of the dark?

Barbara needs a story. A struggling journalist, she tricks her way into the home of former soap star Margaret Reynolds. Desperate for a scoop, she finds instead a terrified woman living alone in a creepy manor house.
A piano plays in the night, footsteps run overhead, doors slam. The nights are full of strange noises. Barbara thinks there may be a child living upstairs, unseen. Little by little, actress Margaret's haunting story is revealed, and Barbara is left with a chilling discovery.

This spooky tale from bestselling author Lynda La Plante will make you want to sleep with the light on.

Quick Reads 📖

Fall in love with reading

Full House

Maeve Binchy

Orion

Sometimes the people you love most
are the hardest to live with.

Dee loves her three children very much, but now they are all grown up, isn't it time they left home?

But they are very happy at home. It doesn't cost them anything and surely their parents like having a full house? Then there is a crisis, and Dee decides things have to change for the whole family . . . whether they like it or not.

Quick Reads 📖

Fall in love with reading

Beyond the Bounty

Tony Parsons

Harper

Mutiny and murder in paradise …

The Mutiny on the Bounty is the most famous uprising in naval history. Led by Fletcher Christian, a desperate crew cast sadistic Captain Bligh adrift. They swap cruelty and the lash for easy living in the island heaven of Tahiti. However, paradise turns out to have a darker side …

Mr Christian dies in terrible agony. The Bounty burns. Cursed by murder and treachery, the rebels' dreams turn to nightmares, and all hope of seeing England again is lost forever …

Quick Reads📖

Fall in love with reading

The Cleverness of Ladies

Alexander McCall Smith

Abacus

There are times when ladies must use
all their wisdom to tackle life's mysteries.

Mma Ramotswe, owner of the No.1 Ladies' Detective
Agency, keeps her wits about her as she looks into
why the country's star goalkeeper isn't saving goals.
Georgina turns her rudeness into a virtue when she
opens a successful hotel. Fabrizia shows her bravery
when her husband betrays her. And gentle La proves
that music really can make a difference.

With his trademark gift for storytelling, international
bestselling author Alexander McCall Smith brings us
five tales of love, heartbreak, hope and the cleverness
of ladies.

Quick Reads 📖

Fall in love with reading

Get the Life you Really Want

James Caan

Penguin

It is possible to get the life you really want.
You just need to change the way you think.

In the thirty years James Caan has spent in business he's learned how to build a very successful company. Using the same business methods, you can build a successful life.

- Discover how to manage your time and money.

- Find out how to set your priorities and communicate well with other people.

- Learn to change how you think so you can use business sense in everyday life.

This ten-point plan will help you achieve your goals, whatever they may be.

Quick Reads 📖

Fall in love with reading

Quantum of Tweed:
The Man with the Nissan Micra

Conn Iggulden

Harper

Albert Rossi has many talents. He can spot cheap polyester at a hundred paces. He knows the value of a good pair of brogues. He is in fact the person you would have on speed-dial for any tailoring crisis. These skills are essential to a Gentleman's Outfitter from Eastcote. They are less useful for an international assassin.

When Albert accidentally runs over a pedestrian, he is launched into the murky world of murder-for-hire. Instead of a knock on the door from the police, he receives a mysterious phone call.

His life is about to get a whole lot more interesting . . .

Quick Reads

Fall in love with reading

Amy's Diary

Maureen Lee

Orion

A young woman finds her way
in a world at war.

On 3rd September 1939 Amy Browning started to write a diary. It was a momentous day: Amy's 18th birthday and the day her sister gave birth to a baby boy. It was also the day Great Britain went to war with Germany.

To begin with life for Amy and her family in Opal Street, Liverpool, went on much the same. Then the bombs began to fall, and Amy's fears grew. Her brother was fighting in France, her boyfriend had joined the RAF and they all now lived in a very dangerous world …

Quick Reads

Books in the Quick Reads series

Quick Reads

Fall in love with reading

Quick Reads are brilliantly written short new books by bestselling authors and celebrities. Whether you're an avid reader who wants a quick fix or haven't picked up a book since school, sit back, relax and let Quick Reads inspire you.

We would like to thank all our funders:

We would also like to thank all our partners in the Quick Reads project for their help and support:

NIACE • unionlearn • National Book Tokens
The Reading Agency • National Literacy Trust
Welsh Books Council • Welsh Government
The Big Plus Scotland • DELNI • NALA

We want to get the country reading

Quick Reads, World Book Day and World Book Night are initiatives designed to encourage everyone in the UK and Ireland – whatever your age – to read more and discover the joy of books.

Quick Reads launches on **14 February 2012**
Find out how you can get involved at www.**quickreads**.org.uk

World Book Day is on **1 March 2012**
Find out how you can get involved at www.**worldbookday**.com

World Book Night is on **23 April 2012**
Find out how you can get involved at www.**worldbooknight**.org

Other resources

Enjoy this book? Find out about all the others from
www.quickreads.org.uk

Free courses are available for anyone who wants to develop
their skills. You can attend the courses in your local area.
If you'd like to find out more, phone 0800 66 0800.

 Don't get by **get on** 0800 66 0800

For more information on developing your skills in Scotland
visit www.**thebigplus**.com

Join the Reading Agency's Six Book Challenge at
www.**sixbookchallenge**.org.uk

Publishers Barrington Stoke and New Island
also provide books for new readers.
www.**barringtonstoke**.co.uk • www.**newisland**.ie

The BBC runs an adult basic skills campaign.
See www.**bbc**.co.uk/**skillswise**